Pippa the Pumpkin Fairy

Sticker Dolly Dress Up

Have fun mixing and matching sticker outfits for Pippa the Pumpkin Fairy and her friends!

•

Find fairy looks to finish each scene and then use the extra stickers to dress the press-out fairy dolls! There are stickers for **standing, dancing, sitting,** and **flying** fairies, as well as **accessories** and **shoes.**

D1119475

make
believe
ideas

Early birds

The fairies jump right out of bed.
They've got a busy day ahead!

Busy bakers

The perfect way to make time fly
is baking lots of pumpkin pie!

Pumpkin patch

The fairy friends have so much fun
watering pumpkins in the sun.

Stormy weather

The fairies don't mind rainy weather –
they love to make a splash together!

Cool by the pool

The fairies chill out at the pool,
with ice-cream treats to keep them cool!

Fairy fix-up

With cans of paint and overalls,
the fairies paint the tree house walls!

Home, sweet
home

Picnic lunch

The fairies eat a picnic spread,
feeling happy and well-fed!

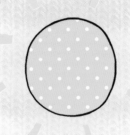

shopping in style

The fairies love to take a tour around the fairy fashion store!

Costume party

As the lanterns gleam and shine,
the fairies' costumes look divine!

BOO!

camping out

The fairies make the air smell sweet
by making yummy, toasted treats!

Flashing fireworks

The fairies gather to watch the sky
as the fireworks flash and fly!

Perfect pumpkins

Pippa makes a pumpkin display –
the perfect end to the perfect day!

Stickers for **Early birds**

Stickers for **Busy bakers**

Stickers for Pumpkin patch

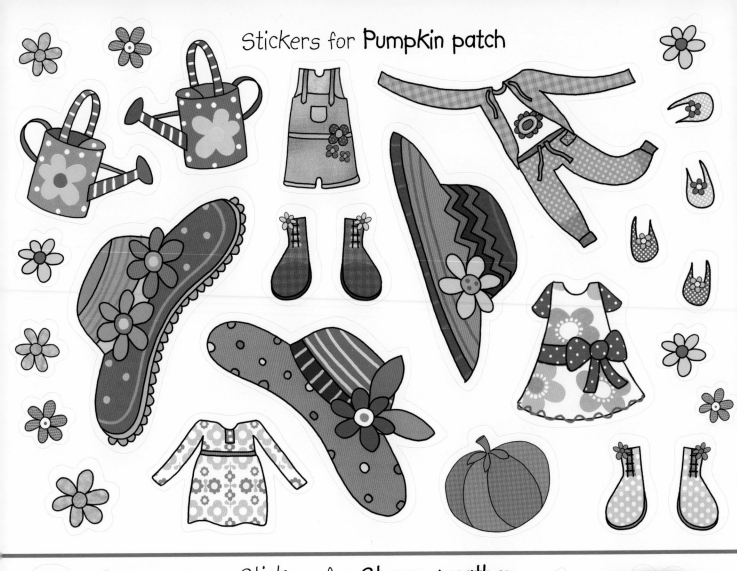

Stickers for Stormy weather

Stickers for **Stormy weather**

Stickers for **Cool by the pool**

Stickers for Fairy fix-up

Shoes for sitting fairy

Stickers for Picnic lunch

Stickers for **Shopping in style**

Stickers for Costume party

Stickers for Camping out

Stickers for Flashing fireworks

Stickers for **Perfect pumpkins**

Extra stickers